The FurFins

If you tiptoe to the shore
and gaze out at the sea,
you might just spot a sparkly tail
or a friendly furry face.
You've just seen a FurFin and found
a very special place.

Shhh, FurFins are real · · ·

The FurFins
and the
Mermaid Wedding

ALISON RITCHIE

illustrated by
ALESS BAYLIS

BLOOMSBURY
CHILDREN'S BOOKS
NEW YORK LONDON OXFORD NEW DELHI SYDNEY

Deep beneath the silvery waves,
nestled in a kaleidoscope of colorful coral,
lies the magnificent kingdom of Coralia.
This is where the FurFins live.

Look—there's StarTail and PosyTail, and over
there by the shimmering seaweed, that's TinyTail!

I wonder what they're
doing today.

StarTail was busy making beautiful headbands with her seahorse Shine.

"I'm so excited," she said. "I can't believe that Princess Coral is getting married today and that we are going to be her bridesmaids!"

PosyTail and her seahorse Sparkle
were making pretty flower bouquets
for the wedding.

TinyTail and her seahorse Boo were
gathering sparkling sea confetti.

"It's going to be the best day
EVER," said TinyTail.
"But there's still so
much to do!"

Meanwhile at her café, CherryTail, the best baker in all
of Coralia, was busy making the royal wedding cake.
Her latest creation was magnificent!

It glistened with silver shells, sugar hearts, and sparkles.
"Ta-da!" said CherryTail as she stepped back to show her seahorse Yum
her handiwork. "A cake fit for a princess! I can't wait to show the others."

StarTail and TinyTail were already on their way.
They chatted happily as they headed for CherryTail's café.

"I bet the princess's cake will look AMAZING!" said TinyTail.

But when they arrived at the café, poor CherryTail was in tears.
"The cake has DISAPPEARED," she cried. "I left it here while I was
tidying up, and when I turned around, it vanished!"

"Jumping jellyfish!" said StarTail.
"Where could it have gone?"

"Don't worry, CherryTail," said TinyTail. "We'll find it.
Let's go and see Ms. Pearl. She always knows how to help."

Ms. Pearl was a great big hug of an octopus. When she saw
the FurFins' gloomy faces, she gave them all a big octo-cuddle.
"Oh deary me," she said. "Why so glum on this happy day, my lovelies?"

CherryTail sobbed. "The princess's wedding cake has been STOLEN!
Who would do such a thing?"

"Well," said Ms. Pearl wisely, "sometimes
when people are feeling sad, they do
things that aren't very nice."

"Who'd be feeling sad on such a special day?" asked
TinyTail. "Maybe we can help them."

"And then we might find the cake, too,"
added StarTail. "Come on, let's go!"

With no time to lose, CherryTail dried her tears and the three friends whooshed off in a whirl of bubbles. They searched the Kelp Forest . . .

and the Sandy Seabed, but everyone was happy and excited about Princess Coral's wedding.

"It's no use." CherryTail sighed. "We'll never get the cake back. The royal wedding is ruined, and it's all my fault!"

But just then, they heard a gentle sobbing . . .

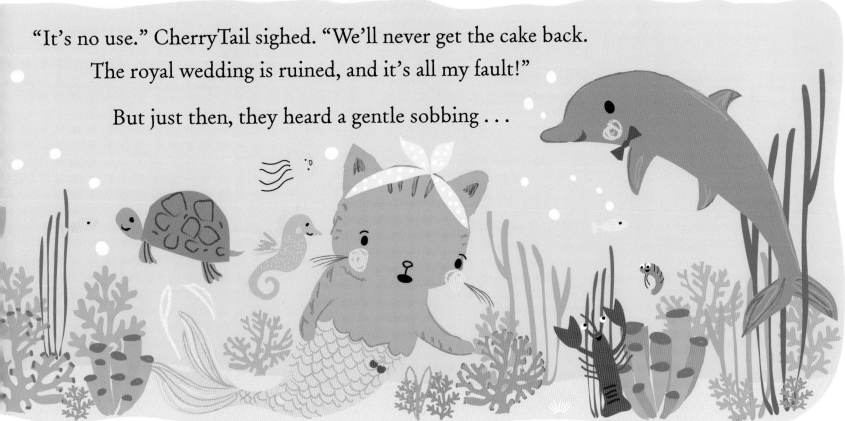

They followed the sound all the way to Ocean Bay, where they found WishTail sitting all alone in the playground.

She was crying her eyes out,
and not even her seahorse Bubble
could comfort her.

"What's the matter, WishTail?"
TinyTail asked gently.

"It's my birthday today," WishTail cried.
"Everyone has forgotten because of the royal wedding."

"I wanted a birthday cake so badly, and when I saw
the wedding cake in the café, I took it . . .

But it didn't make me feel better at all.
I should never have taken it.
I'm sorry!"

And she started crying
all over again.

"Don't cry, WishTail," said StarTail.
"There's still time to make it right."

"Come on, we'll help you!"
said CherryTail.

With a flick of their tails, the FurFins swam off to deliver the cake to the palace, and then hurried back to TinyTail's cove to get ready for the wedding!

Full of excitement, the FurFins put on their special flowery headbands and each of them chose a pretty heart-shaped necklace. But just as they were about to leave, CherryTail looked thoughtful.

"There's something I need to do," she said. "I'll meet you at the palace."

"Okay, but don't be too long," said TinyTail. "You can't be late!"

Back at her café, CherryTail whisked, baked, and iced quicker than she had ever done before.

"All done, Yum," she said.
"Now let's get to the wedding!"

And what a wedding it was!
Princess Coral looked beautiful in her
shining lace dress, and holding up the long,
shimmering train were the bridesmaids . . .

CherryTail,

PosyTail,

TinyTail,

StarTail,

and WishTail!

The happy couple could not stop smiling.
Soon it was time to head off for the wedding feast.

CherryTail had a very special
surprise for WishTail . . .

her very own
birthday cake!

"Thank you all for sharing this special day," Princess Coral said.
"It's someone else's special day too, and we have an important song to sing!"

All the wedding guests sang HAPPY BIRTHDAY
as WishTail blew out her candles and made a wish.

"This is the best birthday EVER!"
she said. "Thank you so much!"

Once everyone had enjoyed the delicious
cakes, they all gathered to wave the prince
and princess off on their honeymoon.

It was the perfect wedding day!
Fireworks popped and sparkled, and everyone
celebrated into the night.

Then with a swish of their tails, the FurFins

...et off together for their next exciting adventure.

For Poppy —A. R.

For Lola —A. B.

BLOOMSBURY CHILDREN'S BOOKS
Bloomsbury Publishing Inc., part of Bloomsbury Publishing Plc
1385 Broadway, New York, NY 10018

BLOOMSBURY, BLOOMSBURY CHILDREN'S BOOKS, and the Diana logo are trademarks of Bloomsbury Publishing Plc

First published in Great Britain in April 2020 by Bloomsbury Publishing Plc
Published in the United States of America in April 2021
by Bloomsbury Children's Books

Text copyright © 2020 by Bloomsbury Publishing Plc
Illustrations copyright © 2020 by Aless Baylis

Bloomsbury books may be purchased for business or promotional use. For information on bulk purchases please contact Macmillan Corporate and Premium Sales Department at specialmarkets@macmillan.com

Library of Congress Cataloging-in-Publication Data
available upon request
ISBN 978-1-5476-0597-2 (hardcover) • ISBN 978-1-5476-0598-9 (e-book) • ISBN 978-1-5476-0599-6 (e-PDF)
LCCN 2020028146

Art created with pencil and Adobe Illustrator • Typeset in Old Claude LP • Book design by Goldy Broad
Printed in China by Leo Paper Products, Heshan, Guangdong
2 4 6 8 10 9 7 5 3 1

All papers used by Bloomsbury Publishing Plc are natural, recyclable products made from wood grown in well-managed forests.
The manufacturing processes conform to the environmental regulations of the country of origin.

To find out more about our authors and books visit www.bloomsbury.com and sign up for our newsletters.

The End